ADLER

FOR RIGHTS INFORMATION CONTACT
jenny.boyce@titanemail.com

ADLER Published by Titan Comics, a division of Titan Publishing Group, Ltd. 144 Southwark Street, London SE1 0UP. Titan Comics is a registered trademark of Titan Publishing Group, Ltd.

ISBN: 9781782760719

A CIP catalogue for this title is available from the British Library.

First Edition March 2021

10 9 8 7 6 5 4 3 2 1

Printed in CHINA.

follow us on twitter@comicstitan | visit us at facebook.com/comicstitan

ADLER

WRITTEN BY:
LAVIE TIDHAR

DRAWN AND COLOURED BY:
PAUL McCAFFREY

LETTERED BY:
SIMON BOWLAND

EDITED BY:
DAVID LEACH

COLLECTION DESIGNED BY
DAN BURA

FOREWORD

"To Sherlock Holmes she is always *the* woman," Dr Watson tells us. Irene Adler was born in New Jersey and became an opera singer and adventuress. In the Holmesian canon she appears merely once – but casts a long shadow.

Doyle had a gift for creating memorable characters who only briefly appear. I have a soft spot for Roylott, the poisoner, who pops up within these pages, as I do for much of popular Victorian literature. When Paul McCaffrey and I set out to write these new adventures of Irene Adler and friends, we drew on a shared love of a Victorian England that was both monstrous and fabulous, an era that was, to reference Dickens, both the best and the worst of times.

Somewhere, then, there is *another* 1902: Queen Victoria still rules, sustained by some terrible science; the forces of colonial resistance gather to fight the British Empire; and Irene Adler and her friends must stop a deadly plot... This is a world of poverty and riches; of science and superstition; it is an unjust world, which is not entirely unlike the world we live in. Our present was shaped by its past.

If I had done one thing it is to write this out of love: for a bygone literature that took delight in thrills and chases, conspiracies and double-crosses, published serially for an audience that only had the written word for comfort. And if I have amused you, as Horace Walpole once said, then I am content.

Lavie Tidhar
London
2020

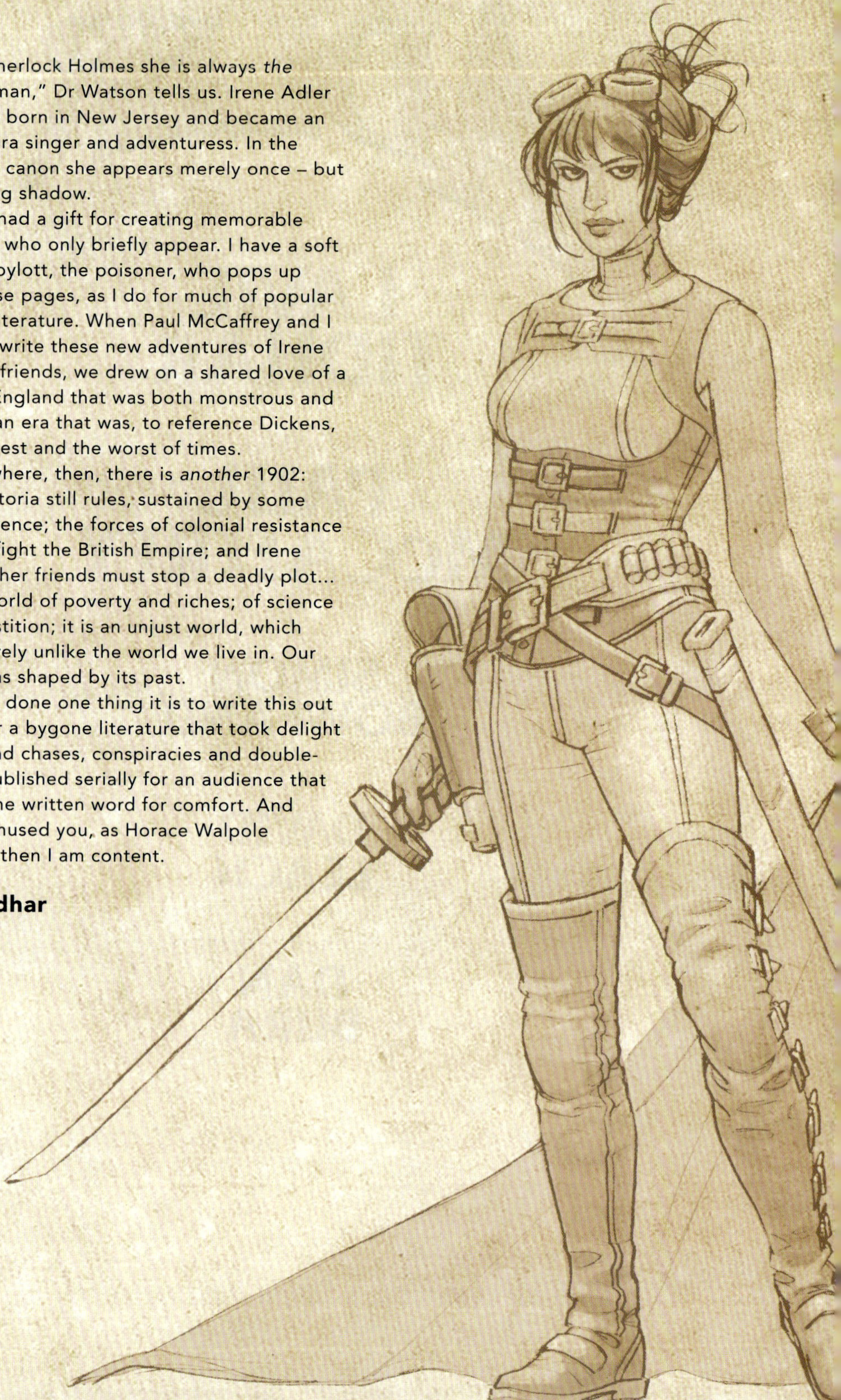

CAST OF CHARACTERS

Irene Adler

Actress, opera singer and adventurer. An American in London. Grew up in New Jersey, which explains a lot, including her familiarity with guns and knife work. Does not tolerate fools gladly.

Lady Havisham

Young socialite and inventor, equally at home in the lab or in the ballroom. Happy to get her hands dirty and never shies from a just fight. Not into marriage.

Jane

Trained as a nurse; served in the Boer War where she was wounded in the line of duty. An honest woman in a corrupt world. Her surname rhymes with "air".

Ayesha

Queen of the Amazons, She-who-must-be-obeyed, Ayesha's righteous hatred of the British Empire which destroyed her home drives her to revenge.

Annie

An orphan. Strong-willed, independent and without fear, Annie has contempt for authority and a love of adventure.

Carmilla

Little is known about the assassin Carmilla, as most people who meet her somehow end up dead. Not someone you want to run into in a dark alley.

Issue#1, Cover B: Paul McCaffrey

SOUTH AFRICA. 1902.
TAKE COVER!
DR. SEWARD! NO!

YOU MUST COME WITH ME, MISS. IT'S CHARLIE! HE'S BEEN HIT. WE MUST HURRY.
I'M A NURSE, NOT A DOCTOR! I --
PLEASE, MISS. WE MUST HURRY.
CHARLIE'S JUST OVER --
THERE...

WHERE? WHERE?
MISS!
MISS JANE? IS THAT YOU?
HENRY? HENRY, IS THAT YOU?
IT'S GOOD TO SEE YOU AGAIN, MISS JANE. BUT YOU MUST COME WITH ME. WE MUST HURRY.
YOU SEE, IT'S... IT'S RICHARD.
MY RICHARD?
HE'S WOUNDED, MISS JANE. WE MUST HURRY!
OH, NO, RICHARD. NO.
JANE... JANEY. YOU FOUND ME.
BLAST IT, RICHARD. DON'T DO THIS TO ME.
ARE YOU CRYING?
NO.
IT'S JUST WAR.

"WOMEN ARE NEVER TO BE ENTIRELY TRUSTED -- NOT THE BEST OF THEM." - SHERLOCK HOLMES.
LONDON.

IN 1902, HAVING SERVED AS AN AMBULANCE DRIVER DURING THE BOER WAR, AND BEEN WOUNDED, AT LAST, IN THE FATEFUL BATTLE OF MAFEKING, I RETURNED TO LONDON, FIVE AND TWENTY YEARS OF AGE, WITH A SMALL SCAR AT THE CORNER OF MY LEFT EYE AS A MEMENTO OF THAT WAR, AND FEW PROSPECTS BESIDES.

LADY HAVISHAM'S RESIDENCE.
SO, DEAR JANE. ARE YOU STILL IN SEARCH OF SUITABLE ACCOMMODATION?
I'M AFRAID SO, LADY HAVISHAM.
JANE HAS JUST COME BACK FROM SOUTH AFRICA.
SOUTH AFRICA?!
I'M AFRAID SO, LADY PENDLETON. SHE WAS AN AMBULANCE DRIVER DURING THE WAR.
ON WHICH SIDE?
ON OUR SIDE, I SHOULD HOPE!
JANE?
I'M AFRAID WE WERE TRYING TO HELP THE WOUNDED AND THE DYING, LADY PENDLETON. WHICHEVER SIDE THEY WERE ON.
I HARDLY THINK --
I BEG YOUR PARDON, LADY HAVISHAM?
QUITE, MY DEAR LADY PENDLETON. WELL PUT.
OH, IT'S QUITE ALL RIGHT, LADY PENDLETON. TELL ME, DEAR JANE, ARE YOU STILL STAYING AT MRS. BROWN'S BOARDING HOUSE IN BAYSWATER?
I'M AFRAID SO, LADY HAVISHAM.

WELL, I HAVE GIVEN YOUR CASE SOME THOUGHT, MY DEAR, AND I BELIEVE I MAY HAVE THE SOLUTION YOU REQUIRE.
MEET ME AT THE *UNIVERSITY* TOMRROW, WILL YOU, JANE? SHALL WE SAY THREE O'CLOCK?
LADY HAVISHAM?
YES, LADY HAVISHAM. THAT'S VERY K--
SOUTH *AFRICA*!
THAT IS NO PLACE FOR A YOUNG *LADY*, SURELY?
I NEVER SAID I WAS A LADY.
I *SAY*!
TEA, LADIES?

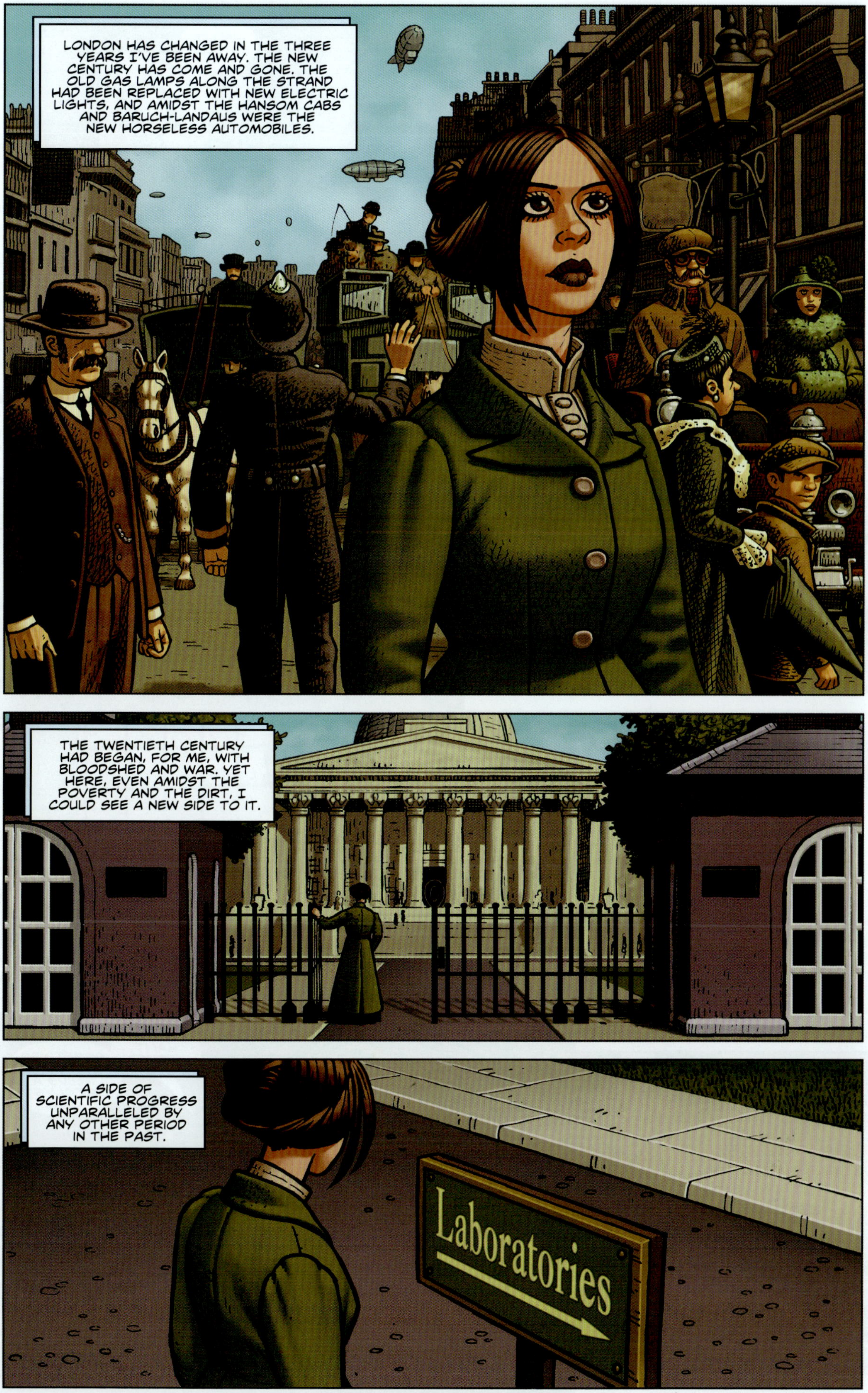
LONDON HAS CHANGED IN THE THREE YEARS I'VE BEEN AWAY. THE NEW CENTURY HAS COME AND GONE. THE OLD GAS LAMPS ALONG THE STRAND HAD BEEN REPLACED WITH NEW ELECTRIC LIGHTS, AND AMIDST THE HANSOM CABS AND BARUCH-LANDAUS WERE THE NEW HORSELESS AUTOMOBILES.
THE TWENTIETH CENTURY HAD BEGAN, FOR ME, WITH BLOODSHED AND WAR. YET HERE, EVEN AMIDST THE POVERTY AND THE DIRT, I COULD SEE A NEW SIDE TO IT.
A SIDE OF SCIENTIFIC PROGRESS UNPARALLELED BY ANY OTHER PERIOD IN THE PAST.
Laboratories

JANE!
HELLO, ESTELLA.
HERE, HOLD THIS.
WHAT IS IT?
ON ITS OWN, IT IS NOTHING. BUT WHEN YOU ADD IT TO THIS --
WELL, GO ON!
NOTHING HAPPENS.
THAT'S BECAUSE YOU NEED A CATALYST.
HA! IT WORKED!
SOMETIMES, EVERYONE NEEDS A CATALYST, JANE.
REALLY, ESTELLA!

COME ALONG THEN, JANE.
WHERE ARE WE GOING?
THERE IS SOMEONE I'D LIKE YOU TO MEET.
COVENT GARDEN.
THERE SHE IS.
WATCH OUT!

HUK!
WHO SENT YOU?

HE... HE DID!
THE PROFESSOR?
Y... YES!
THEN YOU ARE ALREADY DEAD.
YOU JUST DON'T KNOW IT YET.
STAYING OUT OF TROUBLE, I SEE.
JANE, I'D LIKE YOU TO MEET --
ADLER.
IRENE ADLER.
I'M JANE. A PLEASURE TO MEET YOU.
TOMORROW
RENE ADLER
IN CONCERT
LIKEWISE.

YOU ARE A NURSE?
WELL, YES, BUT HOW --
YET YOU HAVE TAKEN ON THE ROLE OF A DOCTOR BEFORE.
YOU HAVE BEEN IN BATTLE AND YOU ARE ONLY RECENTLY ARRIVED IN LONDON.
HOW DO YOU --?
SOUTH AFRICA? OF COURSE. THE BOER WAR. NATURALLY. WHERE YOU LOST SOMEONE DEAR TO YOU, AND RECENTLY. I AM SORRY.
THANK YOU. HOW?
YOUR TAN SUGGESTS YOU HAVE BEEN OVERSEAS, AND RECENTLY. YOU BEAR A SCAR. IT HAS NOT YET HEALED PROPERLY BUT IS CONSISTENT WITH THE WOUND FROM SHRAPNEL. SOUTH AFRICA SEEMS THE OBVIOUS ANSWER.
YOU HAVE THE FAINT SCENT OF ETHER STILL ON YOU, AND AN ALMOST, BUT NOT ENTIRELY, MILITARY BEARING. YOUR HANDS ARE CALLOUSED IN A MANNER CONSISTENT WITH HANDLING SURGICAL BLADES. HENCE, YOU WERE A NURSE, IN THE BOER WAR, BUT TAKING ON THE DUTIES OF A MEDICAL MAN.
INCREDIBLE.

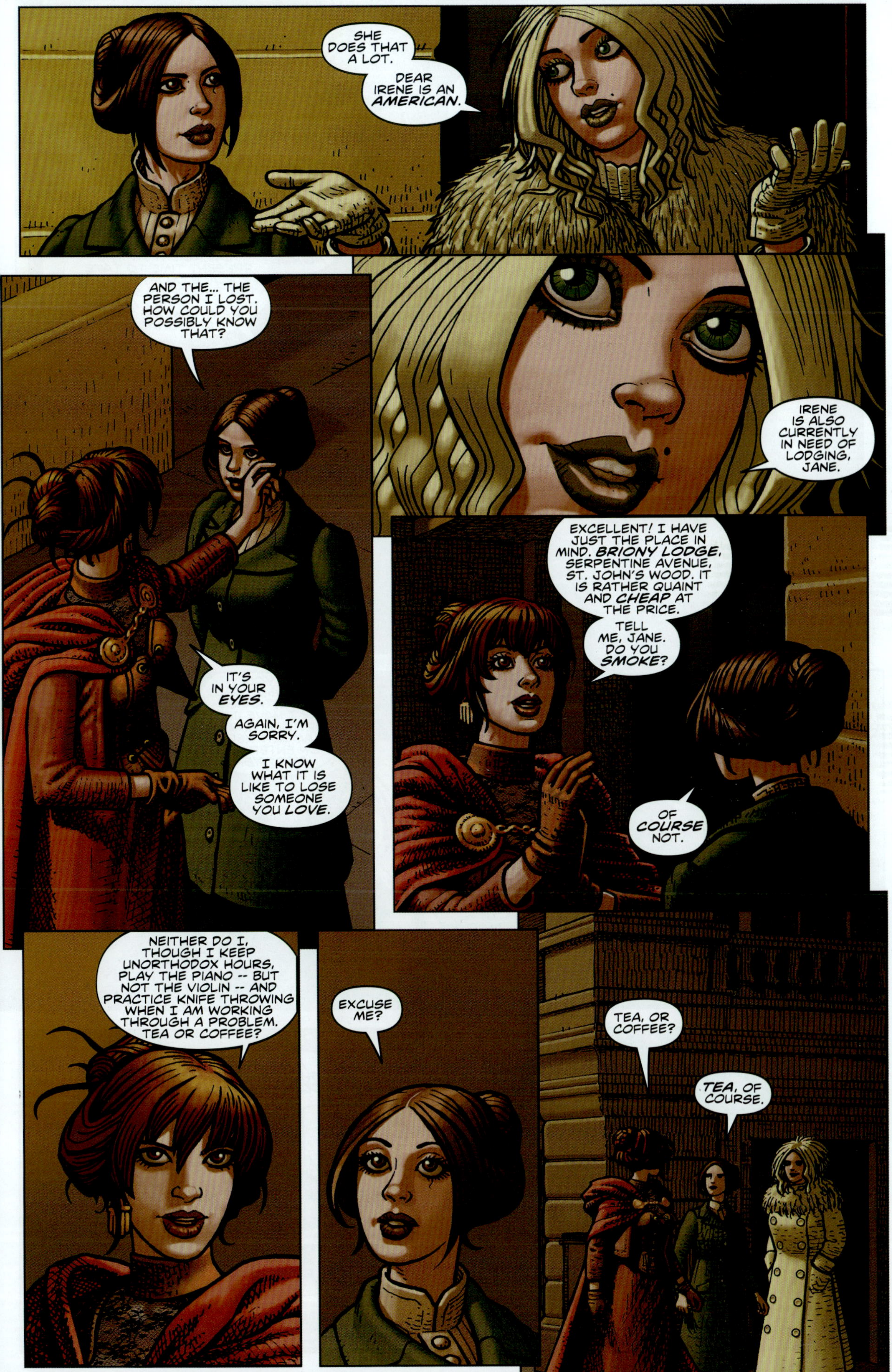
SHE DOES THAT A LOT.
DEAR IRENE IS AN AMERICAN.
AND THE... THE PERSON I LOST. HOW COULD YOU POSSIBLY KNOW THAT?
IRENE IS ALSO CURRENTLY IN NEED OF LODGING, JANE.
IT'S IN YOUR EYES.
AGAIN, I'M SORRY.
I KNOW WHAT IT IS LIKE TO LOSE SOMEONE YOU LOVE.
EXCELLENT! I HAVE JUST THE PLACE IN MIND. BRIONY LODGE, SERPENTINE AVENUE, ST. JOHN'S WOOD. IT IS RATHER QUAINT AND CHEAP AT THE PRICE.
TELL ME, JANE. DO YOU SMOKE?
OF COURSE NOT.
NEITHER DO I, THOUGH I KEEP UNORTHODOX HOURS, PLAY THE PIANO -- BUT NOT THE VIOLIN -- AND PRACTICE KNIFE THROWING WHEN I AM WORKING THROUGH A PROBLEM. TEA OR COFFEE?
EXCUSE ME?
TEA, OR COFFEE?
TEA, OF COURSE.

I NEVER DRINK TEA. ONLY COFFEE. I FIND THAT TEA ADDLES THE SENSES.
I FIND COFFEE DRINKING IS THE SIGN OF AN INFANTILE MIND.
SHE WILL DO, ESTELLA. SHE WILL DO JUST FINE.
IF YOU AGREE?
MY FINANCES ARE INSUFFICIENT AT THE PRESENT TIME TO TAKE THE PLACE ON MY OWN, BUT THE TWO OF US SHARING WOULD DO WELL, AND THE RENT IS MORE THAN REASONABLE.
WHAT DO YOU SAY, JANE?
DO YOU OFTEN GET SHOT AT BY STRANGE MEN? I HAVE JUST LEFT ONE WAR -- I AM NOT KEEN ON ENTERING ANOTHER.
TO BE A WOMAN IS TO BE AT WAR, JANE.
AND I GET SHOT AT ONLY OCCASSIONALLY.
IN THAT CASE, HOW CAN I POSSIBLY REFUSE.

LIMEHOUSE.
THE DOCKS.
WELL?

SHE IS NO WOMAN, PROFESSOR, SHE IS A DEVIL!
SO YOU FAILED.
PLEASE, PROFESSOR...
DO NOT MISUNDERSTAND ME. I AM NOT UPSET THAT YOU FAILED.
YOU'RE NOT?
OF COURSE NOT. SUCH A BLATANT DISPLAY, SUCH A LACK OF FINESSE... OF COURSE IT WOULD FAIL.
SUCH A CLUMSY ATTEMPT WOULD NOT HARM MISS ADLER. IT WOULD MERELY WARN HER.
BUT... WARN HER OF WHAT, PROFESSOR?
WARN HER... OF THINGS TO COME.
FOREKNOWLEDGE IS SOMETHING WE ALL NEED, FROM TIME TO TIME, DON'T YOU THINK?

THEN YOU WILL LET ME GO?
AS I SAID, I AM NOT UPSET THAT YOU FAILED.
OH, THANK YOU, PROFESSOR! THANK YOU!
HKK
I AM UPSET THAT YOU RAN.
CLEAN THAT UP, WILL YOU?
TICKET
IRENE ADLER
IN
LA TRAVIA
THE LONDON OPERA H
7 O'CLOCK

HIS NAME IS MORIARTY. HE IS A PROFESSOR OF MATHEMATICS... AND QUITE THE SCIENTIFIC CRIMINAL MASTERMIND ON THE SIDE.
HE IS NOT AS SIGNIFICANT AS SOME MIGHT MAKE HIM OUT TO BE.
HE IS HARDLY THE NAPOLEON OF CRIME. BUT NEITHER IS HE A GENTLEMAN.
HE TRIED TO KILL YOU, IRENE!
WHAT ARE YOU SAYING?
IF HE WANTED ME DEAD, JANE, I WOULD BE DEAD BY NOW.
I BELIEVE PROFESSOR JAMES MORIARTY IS IN CONSIDERABLE DANGER.
AH. HERE WE ARE!
HELLO, MRS. FLINT.
IT'S CHARMING, MRS. FLINT.
IT WILL DO, WON'T IT, JANE?
IT WILL INDEED.
THE ILLUSTRATED LONDON NEWS
MYSTERY OF THE DEMETER
THE TIMES
CROWN PRINCE WEDS
OH, RUDY...
COLONEL MORAN?
TELL HIM YES.

SIMPSON'S-IN-THE-STRAND.
WELL, COLONEL?
ADLER IS WILLING TO MEET.
I THINK YOUR MESSAGE CAME ACROSS LOUD AND CLEAR, PROFESSOR.
SHE HAS THE PAPERS. I MUST HAVE THEM, SEBASTIAN.
WHAT OF THE OTHER ONE, COLONEL?
SIR?
THE DETECTIVE. THAT LOATHSOME FELLOW AND HIS COMPANION.

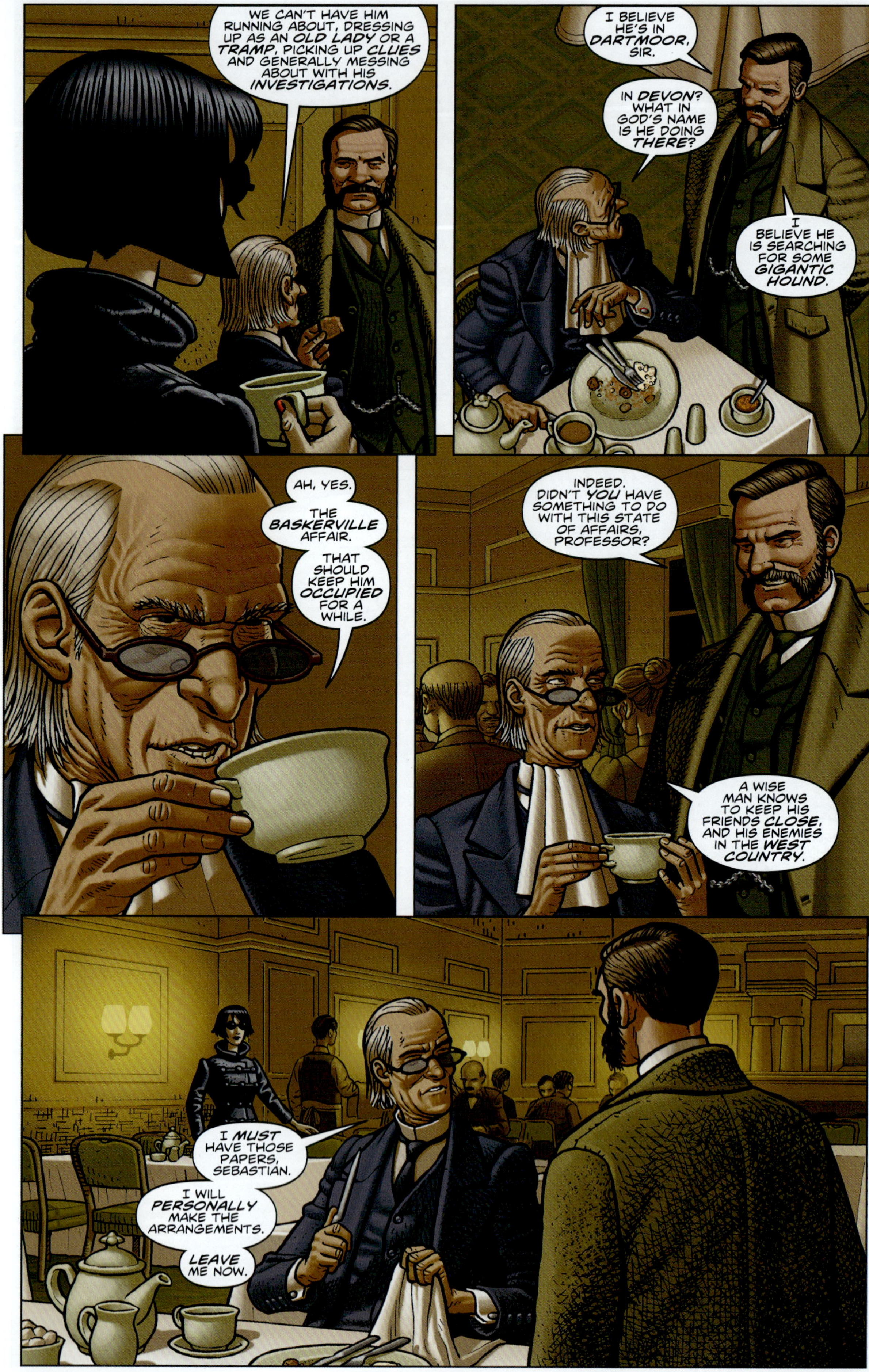
WE CAN'T HAVE HIM RUNNING ABOUT, DRESSING UP AS AN OLD LADY OR A TRAMP, PICKING UP CLUES AND GENERALLY MESSING ABOUT WITH HIS INVESTIGATIONS.
I BELIEVE HE'S IN DARTMOOR, SIR.
IN DEVON? WHAT IN GOD'S NAME IS HE DOING THERE?
I BELIEVE HE IS SEARCHING FOR SOME GIGANTIC HOUND.
AH, YES.
THE BASKERVILLE AFFAIR.
THAT SHOULD KEEP HIM OCCUPIED FOR A WHILE.
INDEED. DIDN'T YOU HAVE SOMETHING TO DO WITH THIS STATE OF AFFAIRS, PROFESSOR?
A WISE MAN KNOWS TO KEEP HIS FRIENDS CLOSE, AND HIS ENEMIES IN THE WEST COUNTRY.
I MUST HAVE THOSE PAPERS, SEBASTIAN.
I WILL PERSONALLY MAKE THE ARRANGEMENTS.
LEAVE ME NOW.

WELL, CARMILLA? REPORT!
YOUR HIGHNESS.
THE PROFESSOR IS MAKING HIS MOVE.
I TRUST YOU TO TAKE CARE OF IT, CARMILLA.
HE MUST NOT OBTAIN THE PAPERS.
OUR AGENTS IN PARIS ARE ON CONSTANT SURVEILLANCE, YOUR HIGHNESS. THE PAPERS WILL NOT LEAVE THE CONTINENT.
GOOD, CARMILLA. GOOD.

LIFE WITH MY NEW FRIEND PROMISED TO BE RATHER *INTERESTING*. IT WAS, PERHAPS, JUST THE TONIC I NEEDED.
I HAD PROMISED TO MEET ADLER THE NEXT DAY, AT THE OPERA HOUSE, WHERE SHE WAS TO SING IN *LA TRAVIATA*. IT WAS THE OPENING NIGHT.
BUT I DETERMINED TO FIND OUT MORE ABOUT HER BEFOREHAND...
PARIS, FRANCE.
"OUR AGENTS IN PARIS ARE ON CONSTANT SURVEILLANCE, YOUR HIGHNESS.THE PAPERS WILL NOT LEAVE THE CONTINENT."
MADAME CURIE
LABORATOIRE DE RECHERCHE
END OF PART ONE.

THE BRITISH LIBRARY. LONDON.
I RESOLVED TO FIND OUT MORE ABOUT MY NEW ROOMMATE. I HAD PROMISED TO MEET HER LATER THAT EVENING, AFTER HER PERFORMANCE. BUT I HAD A LITTLE TIME TO DIG AROUND, FIRST...
AMERICAN PRIMA DONNA TAKES LA SCALA BY STORM
PRINCE RUDOLF OF RURITANI
I HAVE NEVER BEEN HAPPIE
INTERNATIONAL ADVENTURES
FOILS DARING DIAMOND H
RUDOLF OF R
TO MARRY PRINCESS FLAVI
WOMAN OF MYSTERY FOILS SUSSEX VAMPIRE
AMERICAN PRIMA DONNA TAKES LA SCALA BY STORM
MARIE CURIE TIP
FOR NOBEL PRIZE IN PHYS
SHE HAD INTERESTING *FRIENDS*... ADLER WAS FULL OF SURPRISES.
I'M *LATE!*

WHAT'S YOUR HURRY, LITTLE LADY?

THAT SHE-DEVIL! MY HEAD!
MY KNIFE!
AAAGH!
KRRAACK
I'M GOING TO GET YOU, YOU B--
YOU SHOULDN'T SWEAR!
I WALKED AWAY, HURRYING, BUT I FELT I WAS ALREADY TOO LATE. SOMETHING WAS WRONG, AND I DIDN'T KNOW WHAT IT WAS.
IT WAS IN THE LONDON AIR, IT WAS IN THE VERY FOG.

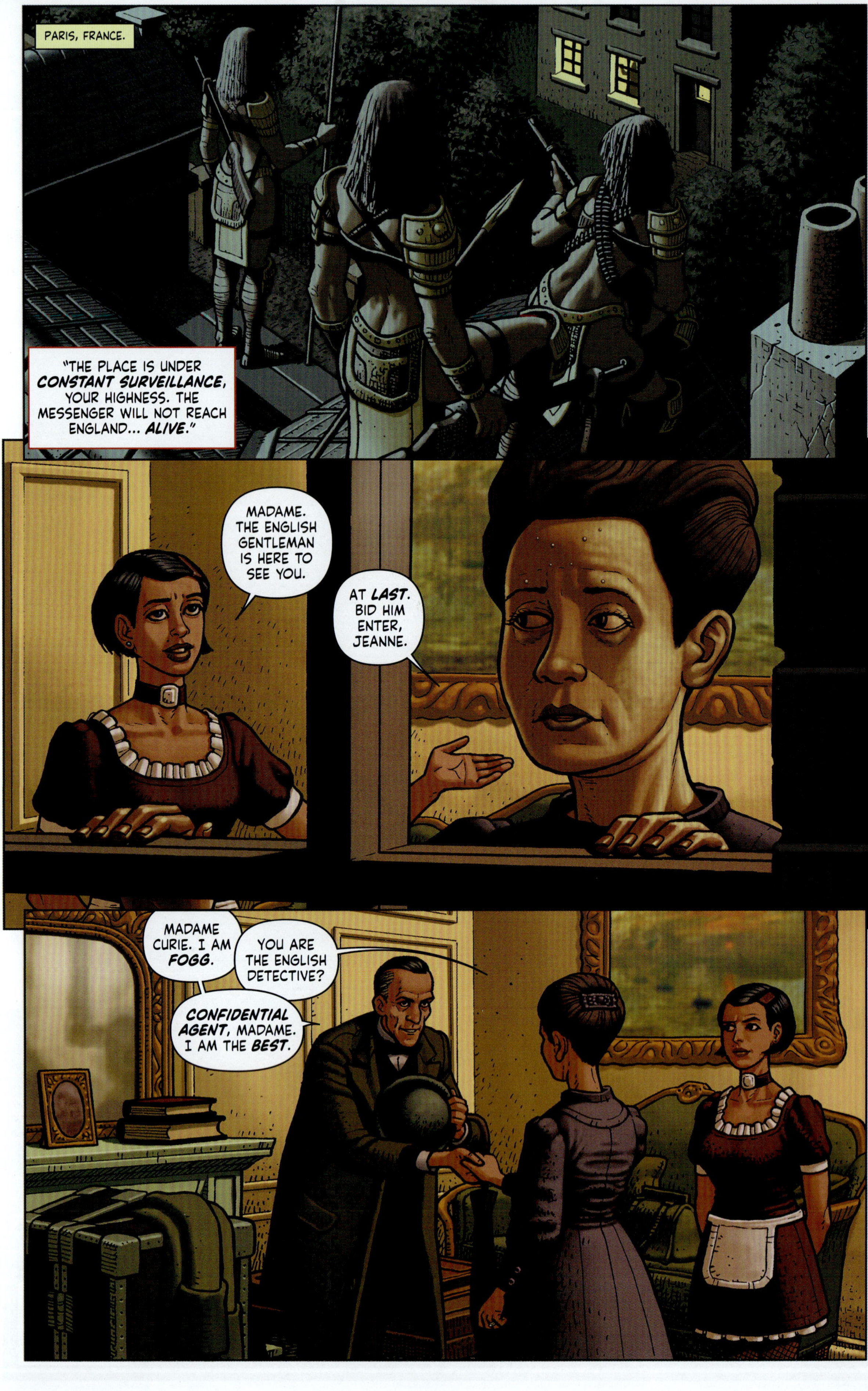
PARIS, FRANCE.
"THE PLACE IS UNDER CONSTANT SURVEILLANCE, YOUR HIGHNESS. THE MESSENGER WILL NOT REACH ENGLAND... ALIVE."
MADAME. THE ENGLISH GENTLEMAN IS HERE TO SEE YOU.
AT LAST. BID HIM ENTER, JEANNE.
MADAME CURIE. I AM FOGG.
YOU ARE THE ENGLISH DETECTIVE?
CONFIDENTIAL AGENT, MADAME. I AM THE BEST.

MR. FOGG, I HAVE A TASK FOR YOU OF THE UTMOST IMPORTANCE.
BUT OF COURSE, MADAME.
THESE PAPERS MUST REACH LONDON, MR. FOGG. THEY MUST DO SO SAFELY, AND THEY MUST DO SO NO LATER THAN TOMORROW.
IRENE ADLER
BRIONY LODGE
SERPENTINE AVENUE
LONDON
ADLER?
YOU MAKE A MISTAKE PUTTING YOUR TRUST IN HER, MADAME. SHE IS NAUGHT BUT A MEDDLING AMATEUR.
I HAVE MY REASONS, MR. FOGG.
VERY WELL! HAVE NO FEAR, MADAME-- YOUR PAPERS ARE SAFE WITH ME.
I BID YOU ADIEU.

I FEAR YOU MAY BE FOLLOWED.
UNLIKELY, MADAM. I AM A MASTER OF DISGUISE!
MADAME, THE MAN IS A FOOL.
FOOLS HAVE THEIR USES, JEANNE.
NOW WE MUST HURRY!
♫
THIS IS THE GIRL?
HER NAME IS ANNIE.
I CAN SPEAK FOR MYSELF.
YOU MUST BE MADAME CURIE. I'VE HEARD OF YOU.
YOU'RE A SCIENTIST.

AND YOU RESEARCH SOMETHING CALLED ***RADIOACTIVITY***.
THAT'S ***ENOUGH***, ANNIE!
I SEE WHAT YOU MEANT, HEADMISTRESS.
SHE'S A STRONG-WILLED GIRL. HER TEACHERS FIND HER ***TRYING***.
I AM ALL THAT YOU SAY. AND I HAVE A ***FAVOUR*** TO ASK YOU, ANNIE. THOUGH IT COULD BE ***DANGEROUS***.
WHAT IS IT?
TO GO TO ENGLAND, TO LONDON, FOR ME. AND TO DELIVER THESE PAPERS TO A FRIEND OF MINE.
HER NAME IS ***IRENE ADLER***.
THE FAMOUS ADVENTURESS?
SHE IS SO ***BRAVE***.
THEY WON'T BE WATCHING FOR YOU... BUT THE DANGER EXISTS.
I WILL DO IT.

THE ROYAL OPERA HOUSE. LONDON.
PROFESSOR MORIARTY. I HAVE THE ROYAL BOX RESERVED.
OF COURSE, SIR.
I BEG YOUR PARDON, MISS.
OH, I AM SO SORRY.
LADIES AND GENTLEMEN, PLEASE MAKE WAY FOR HIS ROYAL HIGHNESS, RUDOLF, CROWN PRINCE OF RURITANIA!

KNOCK KNOCK
COME IN!
RUDOLF? WHAT ARE YOU... YOU CAN'T BE HERE!
IRENE, I... I HAD TO SEE YOU.
IRENE... I AM NOT HERE FOR ME. I AM HERE ABOUT THE PAPERS.
MY... RELATIVE WOULD LIKE TO HAVE THEM. THEIR VERY EXISTENCE IS A DANGER NOT JUST TO THE EMPIRE, BUT TO THE WORLD.
REALLY, RUDOLF. DON'T BE SO MELODRAMATIC.
IRENE, I...
JUST GO!
OH, RUDY...

THE PAPERS, ADLER, YOU CONFOUNDING WOMAN! WHERE ARE MY PAPERS!
CHE MAI DICESTI! MISERA!
AAARRGH!

PIETA TI PRENDA DEL MIO DOLOR!
SIR? YOUR GIN AND TONIC, SIR.
QUEST'AMORE CHE T'IRRITA NELLA TOMBA IO TOM SPEGNERO!
AAAGGHH!

ADLER!
JANE. FOLLOW ME!
HE'S DEAD.
OF COURSE HE'S DEAD, JANE.
DRAT! I'D BETTER LOOK THROUGH HIS POCKETS.
IRENE!
THIS IS PROFESSOR MORIARTY?
THIS WAS PROFESSOR MORIARTY.
WE SHOULD LEA--
LEAVING THE SCENE OF THE CRIME, ADLER? WHAT IS THE MATTER, DID YOU FORGET YOUR KNITTING?
KNITTING'S A NOBLE ART, LESTRADE. ONLY A MAN WOULD BE SCARED OF NEEDLES.

WHAT DO WE HAVE HERE THEN?
ISN'T IT ***OBVIOUS***, LESTRADE? THE DECEASED WAS KILLED WITH A GARROTE, SILENTLY AND PROFESSIONALLY. THE KILLER WAS A WOMAN, FIVE FEET, SIX INCHES TALL AND RIGHT HANDED.
NOTE THE EXTRA PRESSURE ON THE RIGHT SIDE. DO YOU UNDERSTAND? YES?
HOW DO YOU...?
GO ON...
HER PERFUME IS STILL HANGING IN THE AIR. LIGHTLY APPLIED, AND EXPENSIVE. ***NATURELLE BY BERDOUES***, UNLESS I AM VERY WRONG. AND I AM SELDOM WRONG.
ABOUT ***PERFUME***?
ABOUT ***ANYTHING***.
NOW IF YOU'LL ***EXCUSE*** ME, INSPECTOR.
I'M SO AWFULLY SORRY, INSPECTOR.
NOW YOU ***WAIT*** JUST A MINU--
THAT ***BLASTED*** WOMAN!

BRIONY LODGE. LATER.
THWACK
I WAS *AFRAID* THIS WOULD HAPPEN.
I HAD NOT EXPECTED HER TO ACT QUITE THIS *QUICKLY*.
THE GAME IS UNDERFOOT.
YOU MEAN *AFOOT*?
I SAY WHAT I MEAN AND I MEAN WHAT I SAY!
REALLY, IRENE, YOU MUST SETTLE DOWN.
YOU SHOULD EAT. IT IS IMPORTANT TO MAINTAIN A HEALTHY DIET. ESPECIALLY IN TRYING CIRCUMSTANCES.
HOW *DARE* SHE MOVE AGAINST ME!

IN MY OPERA HOUSE! DURING MY PERFORMANCE!
WITH THAT... THAT... ASSASSIN OF HERS!
THE VERY CHEEK OF THAT WOMAN!
WHO?
HER! SHE!
SHE?
IT WAS SHE... SHE-WHO-MUST-BE-OBEYED!
HAVE YOU LOST YOUR MARBLES, ADLER?
SHE DID IT TO SPITE ME.
BUT WHO IS SHE?
"HER NAME IS AYESHA. SHE IS SOME BARBARIAN QUEEN OF A FAR-OFF LAND.
"ONE THAT THE BRITISH EMPIRE FELT SHOULD BE CIVILIZED.
"SHE REFUSED.

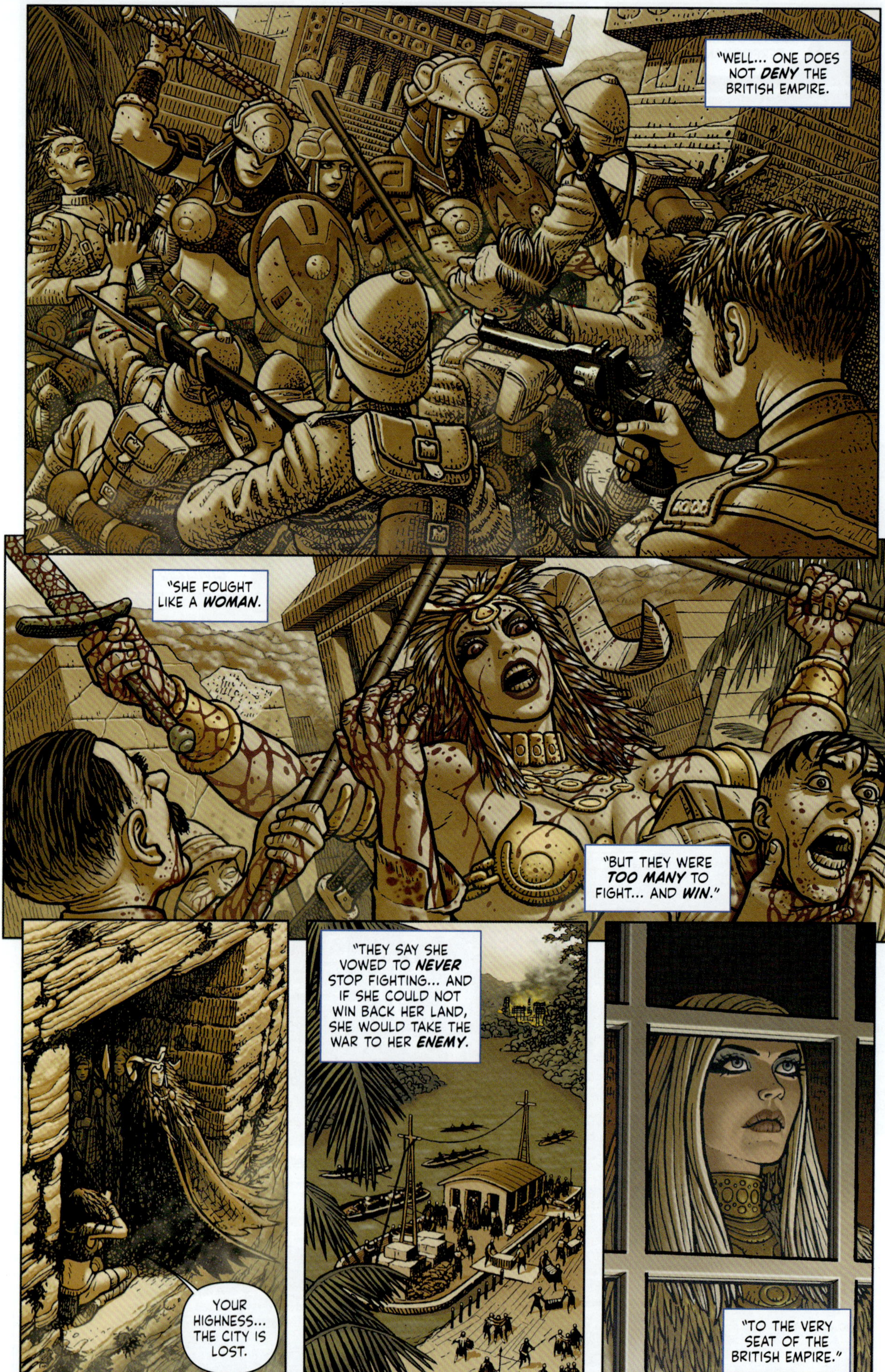
"WELL... ONE DOES NOT DENY THE BRITISH EMPIRE.
"SHE FOUGHT LIKE A WOMAN.
"BUT THEY WERE TOO MANY TO FIGHT... AND WIN."
YOUR HIGHNESS... THE CITY IS LOST.
"THEY SAY SHE VOWED TO NEVER STOP FIGHTING... AND IF SHE COULD NOT WIN BACK HER LAND, SHE WOULD TAKE THE WAR TO HER ENEMY.
"TO THE VERY SEAT OF THE BRITISH EMPIRE."

GENTLEMEN... AND LADIES. THANK YOU ALL FOR COMING.
"TO LONDON."
AIN'T NO LADIES HERE, BEGGING YOUR PARDON, MA'AM.
AH, ROGANA. QUEEN OF THE BEGGARS.
YOURS IS AN ACQUAINTANCE I HAVE LONG DESIRED TO MAKE.
LIKEWISE, MISSUS, I'M SURE.
SPEAK FOR YOURSELF, ROGANA THE FAT!
I AM BELLE, QUEEN OF THE HARLOTS, MADAMS AND DOLLYMOPS!
NOW, WHY DON'T YOU TELL US WHY WE'RE HERE, AYESHA? THE NIGHT IS YOUNG, AND THERE IS WORK TO BE DONE.
SIT DOWN, BELLE. YOU FORGET YOURSELF.
NOW THEN, WHO DO WE HAVE HERE?
WELL IF IT ISN'T ARTHUR RAFFLES, THE GENTLEMAN THIEF.
CHARMED, MY DEAR LADY. CHARMED.

AND, I SEE, DR. ROYLOTT, THE POISONER.
WHAT IS THE MEANING OF THIS!
AND YOU ARE...?
JACK.
JUST... JACK.
JACK. OF COURSE.
RUPERT OF HENTZAU, AT YOUR SERVICE, MADAM.
I HEAR YOU ARE A FINE MAN WITH A SWORD.
AND BETWEEN THE SHEETS!
AND PADDY DOYLE. YOU CONTROL THE DOCKS, DON'T YOU, PADDY?
ENOUGH!
BETWEEN US, WE IN THIS ROOM CONTROL THE ENTIRETY OF LONDON'S CRIME.
NOT A DIAMOND STOLEN WITHOUT OUR KNOWLEDGE, NOT A MURDER COMMITTED WITHOUT OUR NOD.
AND WE ANSWER TO ONLY ONE MAN.
NOW WHERE THE HELL IS MORIARTY?

THE PROFESSOR... HAS BEEN INDEFINITELY DETAINED.
WITH UNDUE PREJUDICE.
MORIARTY IS DEAD?
ASK HER.
THE PROFESSOR WON'T BE JOINING US, I'M AFRAID.
GENTLEMEN-- LADIES--NOTHING HAS CHANGED. ORDER MUST BE MAINTAINED...
THE ONLY DIFFERENCE IS THAT NOW, YOU WILL TAKE YOUR ORDERS FROM ME.
I PROTEST! THIS IS ABSURD! IT IS SIMPLY NOT CRICKET!

A WOMAN? I POISONED MY FIRST WIFE!
PIG!
AND MY SECOND.
RUPERT OF HENZAU OBEYS NO MAN--AND NEVER A WOMAN.
FOOLS!
DO YOU THINK WE ARE GIVEN A CHOICE?
YOU HAVE SERVED YOUR MASTER FAITHFULLY, SEBASTIAN MORAN.
BUT YOUR MASTER IS DEAD.
WILL YOU SERVE ME, NOW?
YES...
I WILL SERVE.

WHAT DO YOU THINK, CARMILLA...
...WILL THEY FALL INTO LINE?
SOME WILL. SOME WON'T. THEY WILL ALL BEAR *WATCHING*. BUT PERHAPS SOME MUST BE MADE AN *EXAMPLE* OF...
DARLING CARMILLA. WHAT WOULD I *DO* WITHOUT YOU?
I DO NOT TRUST THIS *BELLE*.
AND HIM. I DO NOT LIKE THIS SEBASTIAN MORAN.
OH, BUT DEAR COLONEL MORAN CAN BE TRUSTED *IMPLICITLY*, CARMILLA. AS CAN THE LOVELY *BELLE*.
THEY CAN BE TRUSTED TO ACT IN ACCORDANCE WITH THEIR *NATURE*.

YOU ALMOST SOUND AS THOUGH YOU ADMIRE HER, ADLER. THIS AYESHA.
I SUPPOSE THAT I DO. SHE IS RUTHLESS AND CUNNING-- SHE MAKES FOR A FORMIDABLE ADVERSARY.
SOME WOULD SAY SHE IS THE MODERN-DAY LUCREZIA BORGIA OF CRIME.
HELLO. WE SEEM TO HAVE A VISITOR.
BRIONY LODGE
AND THE PAPERS, ADLER?
I FEAR WE MAY BE TOO LATE!
END OF PART TWO

DOVER HARBOUR. NIGHT.
LONDON! LONDON TOWN! ALL ABOARD FOR LONDON!
WHAT'S YOUR NAME, LITTLE LADY?
I'M *ANNIE.* I'D LIKE TO GO TO LONDON.
WHERE ARE YOUR PARENTS?
THEY'RE *DEAD.* I'M AN ORPHAN.
HERE.
CERTAINLY, CERTAINLY, YOUNG MISS... COME ABOARD.

YOU!
SIR?
THEY LET WOMEN DRIVE CABS THESE DAYS?
WHO--?
YOU'RE NO KIND OF DRIVER--!
THEY LET WOMEN DO--
--ALL *KINDS* OF THINGS THESE DAYS!

BRIONY LODGE, LONDON.
TEA, DEAR JANE?
I WOKE UP THAT MORNING FULL OF UNANSWERED QUESTIONS.
YES, PLEASE.
THWAK
I HAD SEEN DEATH, AND DESTRUCTION, BUT HAD NEVER IMAGINED TO SEE THE STREETS OF LONDON AS A DEADLY BATTLEFIELD.
AND NOW I WAS IN THE THICK OF IT. IN THE MIDST OF DANGER.
AND I REALISE THAT I LIKED IT.
THANK YOU.

LONDON, JANE. DOWN HER MEAN STREETS A GIRL MUST GO WHO IS NOT HERSELF M--HELLO, WHAT'S THIS?
COLONEL SEBASTIAN MORAN. THIS IS A SURPRISE.
IRENE ADLER. IT IS AN HONOUR.
LIKEWISE, COLONEL, I'M SURE.
I HAVE COME TO YOU FOR HELP. I KNOW YOU AND MORIARTY DID NOT ALWAYS SEE EYE TO EYE. BUT MISS ADLER--SHE IS BACK!
AYESHA.
SHE-WHO-MUST-BE-OBEYED.

I HAD THOUGHT HER DEAD. IN EIGHTEEN NINETY-SEVEN, IN DAR ES SALAAM.
I MYSELF PULLED THE TRIGGER.
BUT SHE SURVIVED.
I AM BEGINNING TO BELIEVE THE STORIES.
THAT SHE CAN'T BE KILLED. THAT SHE'S IMMORTAL.
NO-ONE IS IMMORTAL. DO YOU KNOW WHAT SHE PLANS?
THE PAPERS.
THE PROFESSOR DIDN'T HAVE THEM BUT SHE--

WATCH OUT!

THE PAPERS, MORAN! WHAT ABOUT THE PAPERS!
AYESHA...
SHE ALREADY HAS THE DOCUMENTS... SHE HAD THEM ALL ALONG!
THAT BLASTED WOMAN!

I HAVE BEEN A FOOL, JANE. WORSE. I HAVE BEEN **COMPLACENT**.
I THINK WE HAVE ANOTHER VISITOR.
A YOUNG LADY TO SEE YOU, MISS ADLER.
SHE SAYS SHE'S COME FROM **PARIS**.
I'M ANNIE. MADAME CURIE SENT ME. ARE YOU MISS ADLER?
I WAS LAST TIME I CHECKED.
I WAS TOLD TO GIVE YOU THIS.
THANK YOU, ANNIE.
THANK YOU VERY MUCH.

RIGHT! WE MUST GO TO HAVISHAM AT ONCE.
ANNIE, JANE, YOU COME WITH ME.
MRS FAIRFAX-- THERE IS A CORPSE ON THE CARPET.
I CAN SEE THAT, DEAR.
SHALL I TIDY UP?
NO.
PLEASE BE SO KIND AS TO INFORM INSPECTOR LESTRADE OF SCOTLAND YARD.
IF HE ASKS AS TO OUR WHEREABOUTS, DO TELL HIM WE HAD A PRESSING ENGAGEMENT IN TOWN.

CHWHAMP
POW
POW
DAMN IT, HAVISHAM, *OPEN* UP!
WHAT IS THE BLASTED WOMAN DOING NOW?

HAVISHAM! WHERE ARE YOU, WOMAN?
ADLER?
REALLY, HAVISHAM!
WHAT WOULD PEOPLE THINK IF THEY SAW YOU LIKE THIS?
FOR A START, I THINK THEY'D KNOW NOT TO STEP ON MY DAMN LAWN.
YOU POOR THING, YOU NEED LOOKING AFTER!
ANNIE HAS JUST COME TO US FROM PARIS, HAVISHAM.
FROM CURIE. ANNIE BROUGHT THE PLANS AT NO SMALL RISK TO HER LIFE.
I WAS RATHER HOPING YOU'D TAKE A LOOK AT THEM.
I SEE. YOU ARE FAMILIAR OF COURSE WITH THE WORKS OF MADAME CURIE?
I AM NOT A COMPLETE IGNORAMUS, HAVISHAM, DEAR.

MADAME CURIE'S RESEARCH IS INTO SOMETHING CALLED **RADIATION.**
INVISIBLE RAYS WHICH ARE ALL AROUND US.
UNFORTUNATELY, SHE DISCOVERED HOW ***DEADLY*** THEY CAN BE TOO ***LATE.***
HER HUSBAND DIED, ***POISONED*** BY THE RADIATION. AND SHE HERSELF IS GRAVELY ILL.
BUT THERE'S WORSE.
WORSE? HOW CAN IT BE ***WORSE?***
CURIE DISCOVERED A NEW ELEMENT CALLED ***RADIUM.*** IF THE ELEMENT IS SUBJECTED TO THE RIGHT TREATMENT, THE RADIATION PRODUCED COULD BE ***MAGNIFIED***--A THOUSAND FOLD! IT COULD CAUSE DEATH...
ON A ***MASS*** SCALE.
THEN THIS--
IF WHAT YOU ARE SAYING IS TRUE--
YES?
THEN THIS MUST BE--
A ***DEATH RAY*** MACHINE?

BEAUTIFUL, ISN'T SHE?
DO THEY ALWAYS NEED TO FOLLOW ME THIS CLOSELY, YOUR HIGHNESS?
AH, DR. TESLA.
AND HOW IS WORK PROGRESSING?
SATISFACTORILY, YOUR HIGHNESS. BUT REALLY, I CANNOT WORK WHEN I AM BEING WATCHED THE WHOLE TIME!
THEY ARE THERE FOR YOUR PROTECTION, DR. TESLA. NOW. HOW IS MY MACHINE?
DOES IT WORK, DOCTOR?
W...WORK? WELL, IT... IT WOULD NEED THE PAYLOAD, OF COURSE.
Y...YOUR HIGHNESS.

THE PAYLOAD?
THE *CRYSTALS,* YOUR HIGHNESS.
MY CRYSTALS! FROM MY VERY OWN *MINES.*
IT IS WHY THE BRITISH QUEEN AND HER GENERALS WANTED TO *ROB* ME.
HELP ME... *WATER...*

"IN MY LANGUAGE WE CALLED IT THE-PLACE-THAT-KILLS.
"ITS VERY AIR WAS POISONED..."
AND THEY DARED TAKE IT AWAY FROM ME?
PRIME THE MACHINE!

WE MUST *TEST* IT, DR TESLA.
T--TEST IT? ON *WHOM?*
AH, *BELLE.*
YOU THOUGHT I WOULDN'T KNOW YOU TALKED TO *IRENE ADLER?* I SEE EVERYTHING, BELLE. AND I FORGIVE *NOTHING.*
LET ME GO, YOU CRAZY OLD BAT!
YOU'RE NOT THE QUEEN OF ME AND MINE. YOU GOT NO... NO *MANNERS.*
SECURE THE TEST SAMPLE!
T...THIS IS MOST *UNORTHODOX,* YOUR HIGHNESS!
WOULD YOU RATHER TAKE HER *PLACE,* DOCTOR?
N... *NO!*

HOW DOES IT WORK?
YOU JUST STAND **HERE**--
--AND PRESS **THERE.**
I GAVE YOU A CHANCE, BELLE. AND YOU BETRAYED ME.
GO TO **HELL,** AYESHA!
HELL IS OTHER PEOPLE, DARLING.
FIRE
IS THIS THING **ON?**
HAHAHAHAHAHA

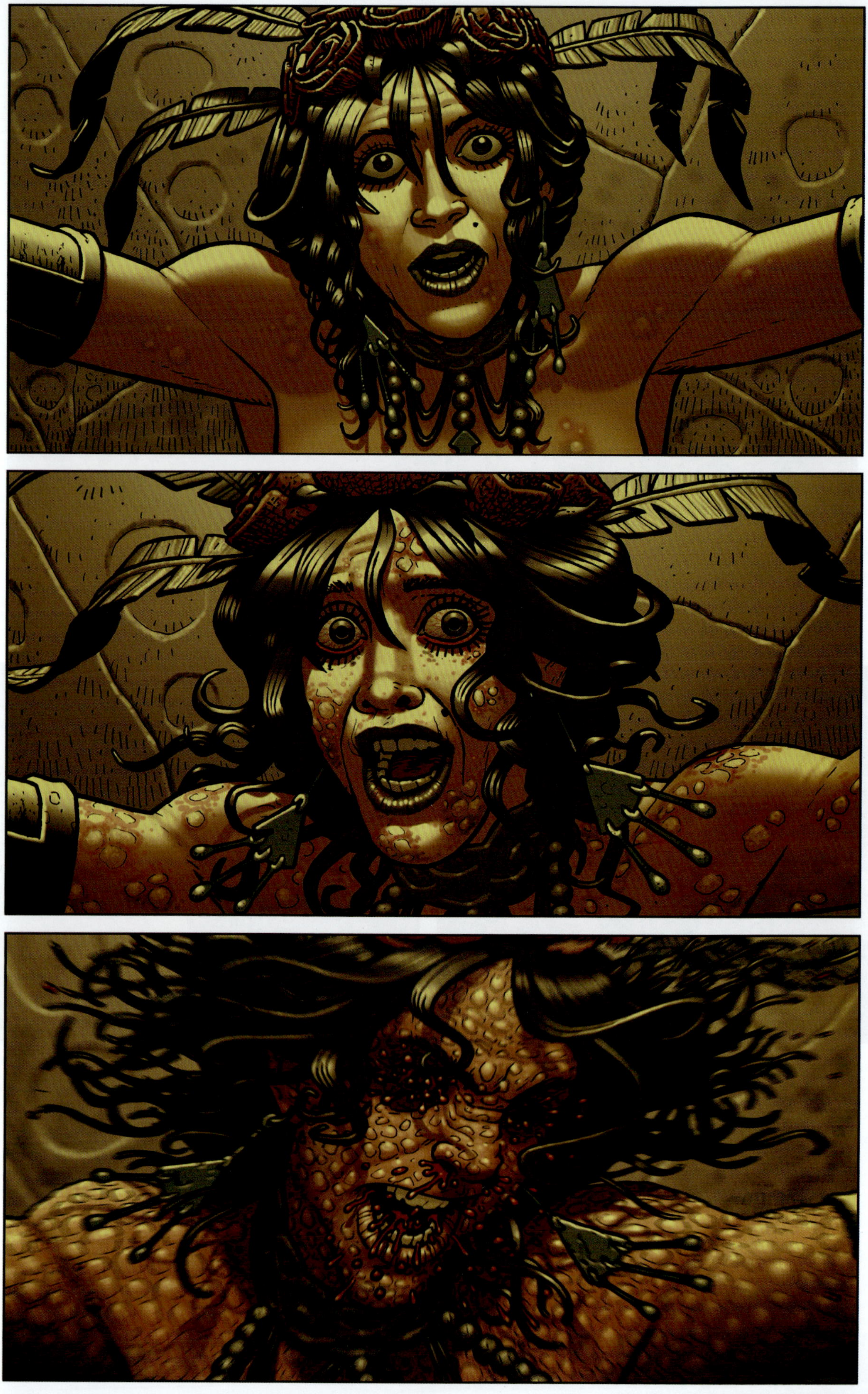

I GUESS IT WAS ON AFTER ALL.

MEANWHILE BACK AT BRIONY LODGE, LONDON.
WELL THAT'S ANOTHER FINE MESS YOU GOT ME INTO, ADLER.
WHAT IS **WRONG** WITH THAT WOMAN!
I WISH **HOLMES** WAS HERE! AT LEAST HE HAS B--
DO TRY TO KEEP THE PLACE TIDY, LESTRADE. AND MAKE SURE TO PICK UP THE GARBAGE ON YOUR WAY **OUT.**
I WILL NOT STAND FOR THIS!
I WANT EVERY AVAILABLE MAN OUT ON THE STREETS. DO YOU HEAR ME?
BRING ME IRENE ADLER!

EXCELLENT WORK, DR TESLA.
WH... WHAT?
ENOUGH, CARMILLA! STOP TOYING WITH THE HELP.
THAT WENT SWIMMINGLY, CARMILLA, MY PET. BUT IT IS NOW TIME TO INITIATE THE SECOND PART OF OUR PLAN.
EXCELLENT, YOUR HIGHNESS.
BUT FIRST, IT IS TIME TO BE DONE ONCE AND FOR ALL WITH THAT INFURIATING WOMAN!
WHAT SHALL WE DO ABOUT THIS BOTHERSOME MISS ADLER?

EVERYTHING IS TAKEN CARE OF, YOUR HIGHNESS.
IN FIVE MINUTES, IRENE ADLER AND HER FRIENDS WILL BE *DEAD!*
END OF PART THREE

LADY HAVISHAM'S RESIDENCE.

WHAT WAS THAT?
STEADY ON, OLD GIRL. IT'S PROBABLY JUST MY MAID.
SHHH...

NO. SOMETHING IS WRONG.
WHAT IS IT?
AMAZONS!

NICELY DONE, JANE!
I WAS SLOPPY--AND NOW AYESHA IS MAKING HER MOVE AGAINST ME. AGAINST US.
TOO SOON!

THEY DARE ATTACK ME IN MY OWN HOME?
WE NEED ARMS, HAVISHAM!
WELL THEN, MY DEAR ADLER--
--YOU'VE COME TO THE RIGHT PLACE!
IS THIS REALLY NECESSARY?

LOCK AND LOAD, LADIES!

WATCH THE BLASTED *CARPETS*!
I JUST HAD THEM *CLEANED*.

KRASH
SO.
LET'S GET TO IT.

IF WE COULD JUST MAKE IT TO THE DOOR!

OH.
WE SEEM TO HAVE MADE A BIT OF A MESS OF YOUR HOUSE, HAVISHAM.
NONSENSE, ADLER. IT WAS BEYOND TIME TO REDECORATE ANYWAY.

TELL MY COUSIN I SHALL SEE HER SOON.
COME WITH ME, ANNIE. YOU MUST BE HUNGRY AFTER ALL THIS EXCITEMENT.
WELL, THAT WAS JOLLY!

YOUR MAJESTY!
YOU... YOU LOOK JUST LIKE IN YOUR STAMPS.
I SHOULD HOPE NOT!
I AM OLD BEYOND MY YEARS, AND HANGING ON TO LIFE BY A THINNING THREAD. BUT I WILL NOT GO WHILE THAT WOMAN TRIES TO USURP ME!
COMING OUT HERE, IN PERSON, WAS TOO DANGEROUS, YOUR MAJESTY. YOU SHOULD NOT HAVE COME.
YOU THINK TO INSTRUCT ME, MISS ADLER? YOU FORGET YOUR PLACE.
I NEED TO KNOW JUST ONE THING...
WHAT IS AYESHA PLANNING?

BUT WHAT ABOUT THE *MACHINE*?
FORGET THE MACHINE, DR. TESLA. IT IS NOTHING BUT A ***DISTRACTION***.
THE EGYPTIAN HALL. PICCADILLY. TWO HOURS EARLIER.
HELLO, SAILOR.
BUT... BUT WHAT IS SHE PLANNING TO ***DO***?

THE POOR *CREATURES*. I WOULD SET THEM FREE, DR. TESLA.
THEY WOULD HAVE CAGED ME LIKE THEY DO THESE UNFORTUNATES, AND CHARGED A PRETTY PENNY FOR IT, TOO.
ONLY A PENNY FOR A POP!
EXHIBITION

OF COURSE! HOW COULD I BE SO BLIND!
IT WAS NEVER ABOUT THE DEVICE. SHE DOES NOT PLAN AN ASSASSINATION, YOUR MAJESTY--SHE INTENDS TO COMMIT MASS SLAUGHTER!

ELEGRAPH OFFICE
H. H. CRIPPEN APOTHECARY
THE QUEEN
THE QUEEN'S HEAD
We carry the 7% Solution!
TO THE HENDRON AERODROME!

BEEEEEP BEEP BEEP
BEEP
BEEEEEP
BEEEEEP
BEEP
BEEP
BEEP
BEEEEEP
BEEP
ME DANGER STOP CLOSE AERODROME IMMEDIATELY STOP PREPARE FOR ATTACK STOP BY ORDER OF HER MAJESTY THE

MAGNIFICENT, ISN'T SHE?
THE VICTORIA IS THE FINEST FLYING MACHINE IN THE WORLD, YOUR HIGHNESS. BUT THERE IS A PARTY ON BOARD, READY TO LEAVE! YOU CAN'T...
BRING HER DOWN!

I SAY! THIS IS *PREPOSTEROUS*! WHAT IS THE MEANING OF THIS!
RUDOLF! WHO ARE THESE PEOPLE? WHAT DO THEY WANT?
CARMILLA? CARMILLA!
SUBDUE THE PASSENGERS, WILL YOU?
PLEASE ESCORT DR TESLA ON BOARD.
OH, AND DOCTOR?
PLEASE DON'T FORGET MY *BOMB*.

COME WITH ME, MISS.
DON'T YOU DARE LAY YOUR HANDS ON HER!
DON'T MOVE IF YOU VALUE YOUR LIFE.
OOF!
WHAT... WHAT KIND OF WOMAN **ARE** YOU!
THE KIND THAT KEEPS MEN LIKE YOU **AWAKE** AT NIGHT.
WHAT DO WE HAVE HERE?
PRINCE...NO, **KING** RUDOLF OF RURITANIA, IF I AM NOT MISTAKEN? AND HIS NEW BRIDE, **FLAVIA**.
HOW... **INTERESTING**.

THIS IS THE WOMAN HE SWAPPED IRENE ADLER FOR?
HOW EXTRAORDINARY.
ESCORT OUR GUESTS ON BOARD.
TAKE HER UP!
AND SET UP THE BOMB...

WE'RE TOO LATE!
WE... WE LOST.
I NEVER LOSE!
HURRY!
END OF PART FOUR

FOLLOW THAT AIRSHIP!
IRENE?
RUDOLF!
KRAK
OH, RUDOLF...

NDON
DROME
A BOMB, ADLER HAD SAID. A DIRTY BOMB, FULL OF RADIOACTIVE MATERIAL, READY TO BLOW AND SHOWER THE CITY WITH DEATH.
TOO LATE. WE ARRIVED TOO LATE.
IRENE...

IT IS DONE.

I *TOLD* YOU, JANE.
I *NEVER* LOSE!
COME ON!

WELL?
IT IS ALMOST READY, YOUR HIGHNESS. BUT WE NEED TO CLIMB HIGHER.
PREPARE FOR LAUNCH, DR TESLA. LONDON WILL BE DESTROYED!
FAIL ME, AND YOURS WILL MERELY BE THE FIRST CORPSE...
FIRE AT WILL!
AYE AYE, CAPTAIN!

HOW... HOW *DARE* SHE! *KILL THEM!*
WE LIVE OR WE DIE, JANE!
I'M TOO YOUNG TO DIE!
STOP THEM, CARMILLA!

THUD
KRRRK
YOU!
IRENE! HELP!
RUDOLF?

RUDOLF!
YOU CAN HANDLE HER, JANE. I MUST SAVE HIM!
WAIT...!
IT'S READY.
0200
0159

WHAT WILL YOU DO, IRENE ADLER?
SAVE YOUR LOVE, OR SAVE THE WORLD?
015
0148

ADLER!
KRAK

IRENE... YOU CAME.
DON'T MOVE!
OH, RUDY.
IT COULD NEVER BE, BETWEEN US.
IN CASE WE DON'T MAKE IT.
0121

FOOLS!
ABANDON SHIP! ABANDON SHIP, MY AMAZONS!
PRAY FOR A QUICK DEATH, ADLER!
0059

WE HAVE TO BRING HER DOWN!
WHAT'S OUR BEARING?
SOUTH WEST, TO SURREY--
BUT WE'RE NOT GOING TO MAKE IT!
WE HAVE TO TRY!
COME ON!
0030

0015
HORSELL COMMON

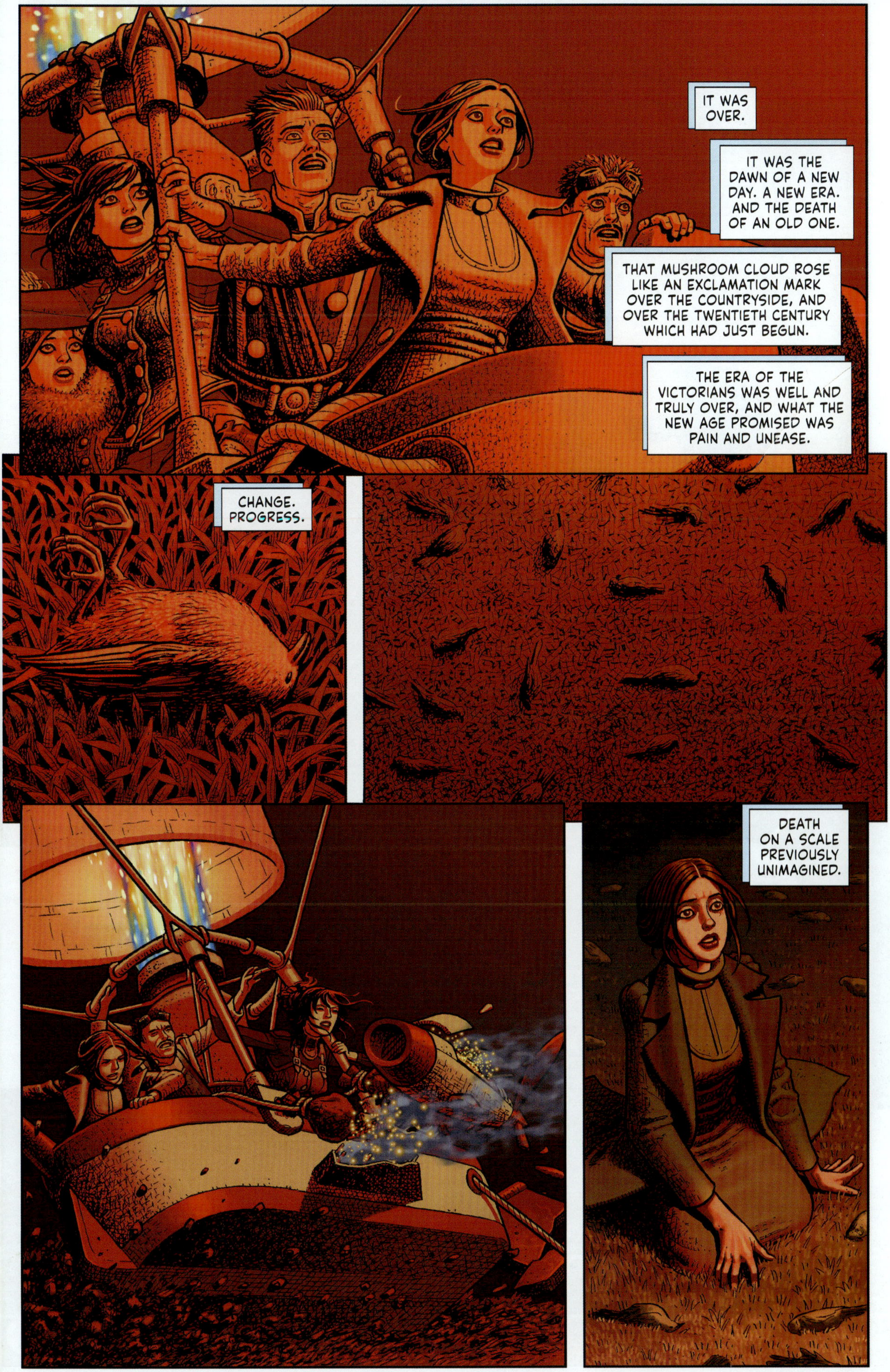
IT WAS OVER.
IT WAS THE DAWN OF A NEW DAY. A NEW ERA. AND THE DEATH OF AN OLD ONE.
THAT MUSHROOM CLOUD ROSE LIKE AN EXCLAMATION MARK OVER THE COUNTRYSIDE, AND OVER THE TWENTIETH CENTURY WHICH HAD JUST BEGUN.
THE ERA OF THE VICTORIANS WAS WELL AND TRULY OVER, AND WHAT THE NEW AGE PROMISED WAS PAIN AND UNEASE.
CHANGE. PROGRESS.
DEATH ON A SCALE PREVIOUSLY UNIMAGINED.

BUCKINGHAM PALACE.
MYCROFT... WELL?
THE NEWSPAPERS WILL DEMAND AN EXPLANATION, YOUR HIGHNESS.
TELL THEM... TELL THEM IT WAS A MARTIAN INVASION.
WOKING IS BEING EVACUATED. THE SURVIVORS ARE BEING PLACED IN A SECURE... CAMP, BY THE SEASIDE.
YOUR HIGHNESS. IT IS TIME.
DR. JEKYLL... HOW WOULD I LIVE WITHOUT YOU?
YOU WOULDN'T.

CHARING CROSS STATION. THE STRAND.
THAT AWFUL WOMAN!
THAT WOMAN SAVED OUR LIVES, FLAVIA.
THAT WOMAN, THAT WOMAN, THAT WOMAN!
I--
IRENE?

GUY'S HOSPITAL.
I RETURNED TO MY JOB. IT WAS AS THOUGH NOTHING HAD HAPPENED.
IT WAS OVER AND THE CITY WAS SAVED. AND YET SOMEHOW IT FELT AS THOUGH WE WERE STILL WAITING.
JANE! HURRY!
LADY HAVISHAM TOOK A SHINE TO ANNIE. SHE WAS BRINGING HER UP TO BE A LADY...
AT LEAST, BY LADY HAVISHAM'S STANDARDS.
AYESHA WAS NEVER FOUND.
BUT I EXPECTED WE HAD NOT HEARD THE LAST OF HER YET.

AS FOR MORIARTY'S RAGTAG CREW...
GENTLEMEN. MORIARTY IS DEAD AND AYESHA IS LOOSE, BUT THE EMPIRE OF CRIME MUST CONTINUE.
HEAR, HEAR!
GOD SAVE THE QUEEN!
GOOD NIGHT, JANE.
GOOD NIGHT, EMMA.
AND SO IT FELT TO ME AS THOUGH THE NIGHT WAITED, AS THOUGH I WAITED.
FOR SOMETHING TO END, OR TO BEGIN.
QUICK, JANE! WE MUST HURRY!
BUT WHERE ARE WE GOING?
HAVE YOU HEARD OF THE EMPRESS-DOWAGER CIXI?

LIMEHOUSE.
MY WARD, THE GUANGXU EMPEROR... HE WAS VISITING LONDON, IN SECRET. NO ONE KNEW OF HIS VISIT, WHICH WAS OF THE UTMOST IMPORTANCE. IT IS A MATTER OF STATE.
HE HAS BEEN KIDNAPPED.
THE FUTURE OF CHINA ITSELF LIES IN THE BALANCE, MISS ADLER.
I NEED YOUR HELP.
SAY WHAT YOU LIKE OF IRENE ADLER...
BUT LIFE WITH HER WAS SELDOM UNEVENTFUL.
THE END

COVER GALLERY

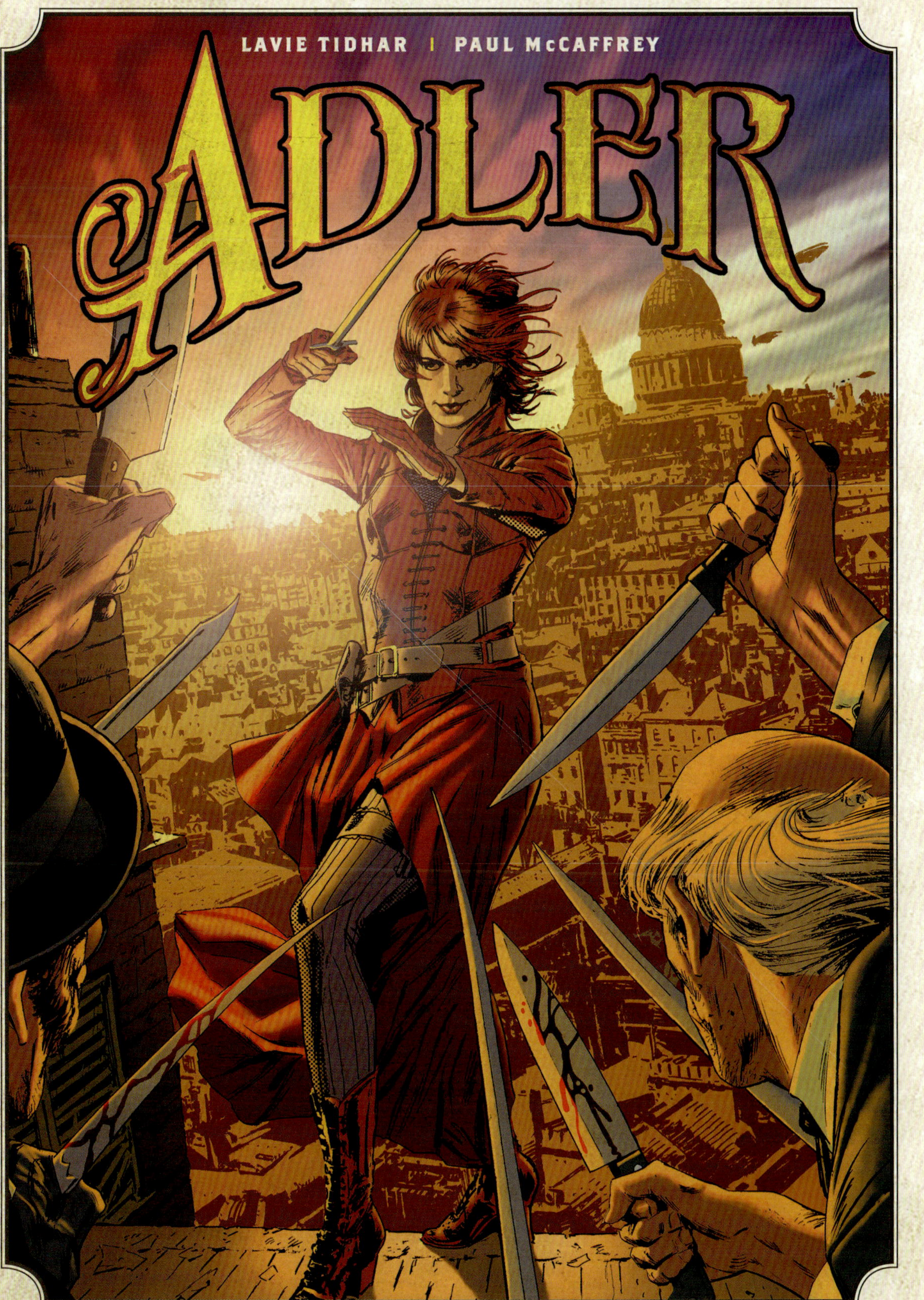

Issue#1, Cover A: Butch Guice

Issue#2, Cover A: Christian Ward

Issue#2, Cover B: Paul McCaffrey

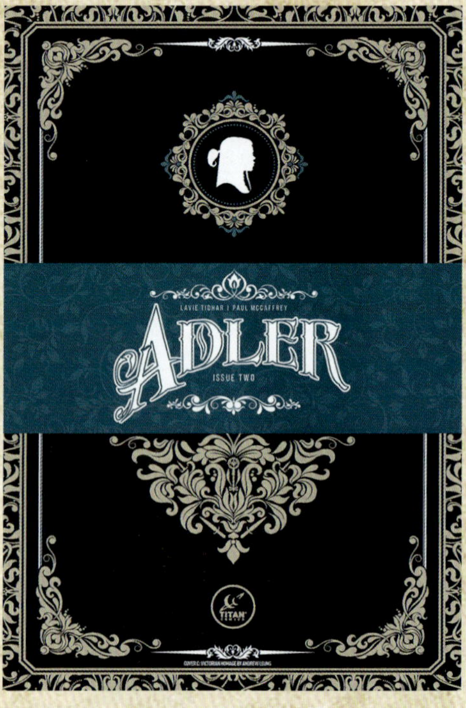

Issue#2, Cover C: Andrew Leung

Issue#3, Cover A: Rian Hughes

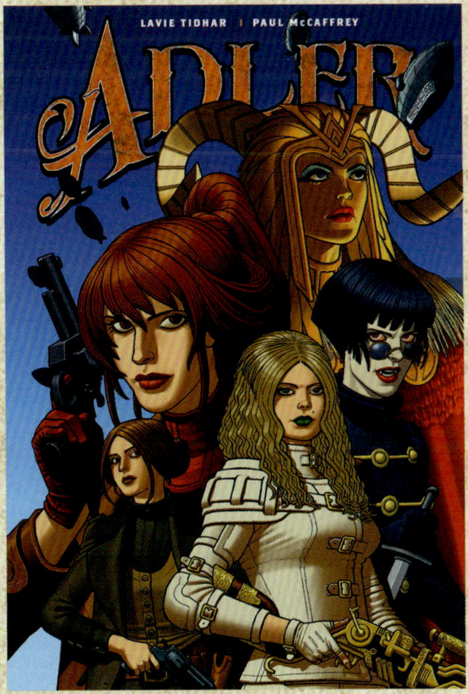

Issue#3, Cover B: Paul McCaffrey

Issue#3, Cover C: Andrew Leung

Issue#4, Cover A: John Royle/James Offredi

Issue#4, Cover B: Paul McCaffrey

Issue#4, Cover C: Andrew Leung

Issue#5, Cover A: Gary Erskine

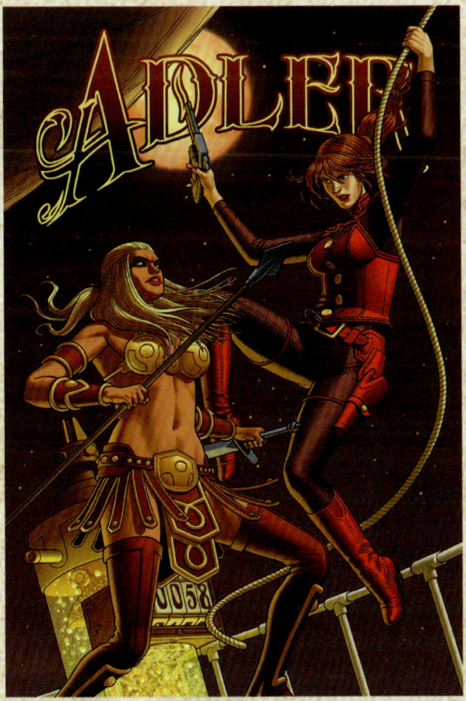

Issue#5, Cover B: Paul McCaffrey

Issue#5, Cover C: Andrew Leung

THE PAUL McCAFFREY FEMALE CHARACTERS GALLERY

Presented here are a selection of artist Paul McCaffrey's designs for the female characters of Adler.

Adler ▸

A selection of proposed outfits for our heroine from modest attire to be worn at an afternoon tea-party to full-on warrior mode.

◂ Ayesha

Early approach for She Who Must be Obeyed, mirroring the tailored armour of Adler.

Carmilla

Ayesha's right hand woman, and vampire to boot.

Miss Havisham

McCaffrey initially pictured Miss Havisham as totally unhinged and wanted her attire to reflect this, however he soon demurred to this more measured approach.

Jane Eyre

Seen here in both skirt and jodhpurs. Although in real life, woman would not start wearing jodhpurs until the 1920s.

THE PAUL McCAFFREY
MALE CHARACTERS GALLERY

This second visit to the gallery of Paul McCaffrey sees his designs for the secondary male characters from the world of Adler.

Moriarty

The Napoleon of Crime. McCaffrey's early take on Moriarty was subsequently tweaked to make him look far more sinister and ruthless.

Grimesby Roylott

A one-time adversary of Sherlock Holmes, Grimesby Roylott was originally described as a 'huge, intimidating figure with a large face, seared with a thousand wrinkles' by Sir Arthur Conan Doyle.

Rupert of Hentzau

Rupert of Hentzau – the dashing and disgraced Count of Hentzau who once imprisoned the King of Ruritania in the castle of Zenda.

Raffles

Arthur J. Raffles, gentleman thief and cricketer, known by all as the Amateur Cracksman. A master of disguise and a great mimic of regional accents.

Sebastian Moran

Two different versions of 'the second most dangerous man in London' and Professor Moriarty's right hand man and chief of staff. McCaffrey went for the handlebar moustache over the more rugged and brutal looking man in the sketch above.

Jack

Jack resembles a young David Warner, the actor who played Jack the Ripper in the movie *Time After Time* battling against that other Victorian, H.G. Wells.

BIOS

Lavie Tidhar

Lavie Tidhar is author of *Osama, The Violent Century, A Man Lies Dreaming, Central Station*, and *Unholy Land*, as well as the *Bookman Histories* trilogy. His latest novels are *By Force Alone, The Escapement* and children's book *The Candy Mafia.* His awards include the World Fantasy Award, the British Fantasy Award, the John W. Campbell Award, the Neukom Prize and the Jerwood Fiction Uncovered Prize. *Adler* is his first graphic novel.

Paul McCaffrey

Paul McCaffrey is a freelance illustrator and cartoonist. His illustration clients have included *NME, Vox, Punch, Deadline, Empire*, Macmillan, Harcourt and Heinemann His first comics work appeared in *Omnivistascope* and he has subsequently drawn *Men of War, Cory Doctorow's Futuristic Tales of The Here And Now, Vote Loki, Fawkes of the Air Ministry*, and *TV21, Captain Scarlet*, and *Joe 90* for Network Distribution. For Titan Comics, he drew Kim Newman's mini-series *Anno Dracula 1895: Seven Days in Mayhem*. He previously collaborated with Lavie Tidhar on the children's book *Going To The Moon*.